BRANDON'S SO BOSSY!

Written by Judith Heneghan

Illustrated by Jack Hughes

WINDMILL
BOOKS™

New York

Published in 2016 by **Windmill Books**,
An Imprint of Rosen Publishing
29 East 21st Street, New York, NY 10010

Commissioning Editor: Victoria Brooker
Design: Lisa Peacock and Alyssa Peacock

Library of Congress Cataloging-in-Publication Data

Heneghan, Judith.
Brandon's so bossy! / by Judith Heneghan.
p. cm. — (Dragon school)
Includes index.
ISBN 978-1-4777-5603-4 (pbk.)
ISBN 978-1-4777-5602-7 (6 pack)
ISBN 978-1-4777-5526-6 (library binding)
1. Etiquette for children and teenagers — Juvenile fiction.
2. Dragons — Juvenile fiction. I. Heneghan, Judith, 1965-. II. Title.
PZ7.H437 Br 2016
395.1—d23

Manufactured in the United States of America

CPSIA Compliance Information: Batch #WS15WM: For Further Information contact Windmill Books, New York, New York at 1-866-478-0556

CONTENTS

Brandon wasn't the biggest dragon at Dragon School, but he was the bossiest. He loved telling his friends what to do.

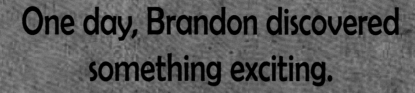

One day, Brandon discovered
something exciting.

Dragon

Skills

Contest

"The Dragon Skills Contest is tomorrow!"
he told his friends. "There are prizes for flying,
roaring, and fire breathing!"

Dragon

Skills

Contest

"Yippee!" said Jasmine.
"I love flying! Let's practice!"
"Ooh yes!" agreed Noah and Ruby.

The three young dragons flew up towards
the clouds. They twirled and they swooped.
Jasmine even looped the loop.

"Come and join us, Brandon!"
she called as she hovered overhead.
But Brandon was frowning.

"Stop!" he shouted, bossily, zooming up in front of them. "Your flying is all wrong! You're not doing it properly! Follow me!"

So the other three dragons stopped twirling
and swooping and loop-dee-looping,
and followed Brandon.

Brandon flew in straight lines, back and forth, back and forth, back and forth.

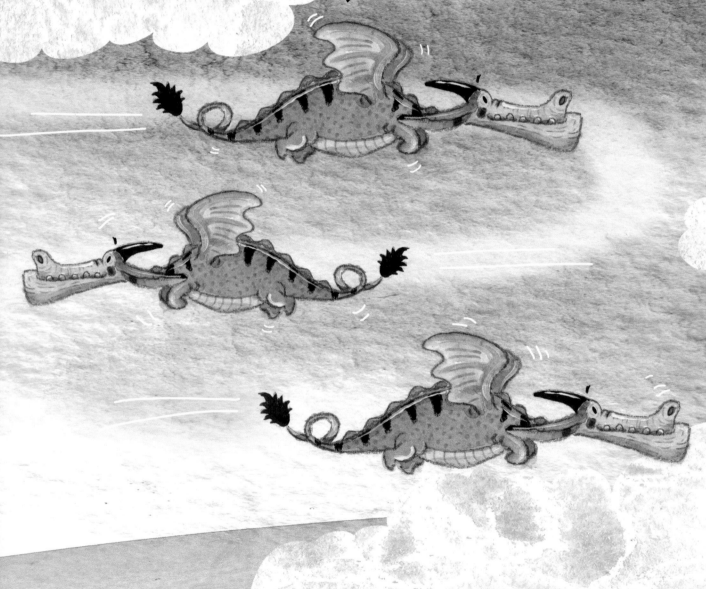

"This isn't much fun," said Jasmine.
"I'd rather practice roaring," said Noah.
"So would I!" agreed Ruby.

Noah flew down to the ground and took a deep breath. "ROOAARR!" he roared, as loudly as he could. Jasmine and Ruby did the same.

RROOARRR!

Their roars echoed around the mountains.
"Wow, that sounds good," said Noah.
"Come and join us, Brandon!"
But Brandon was annoyed.

15

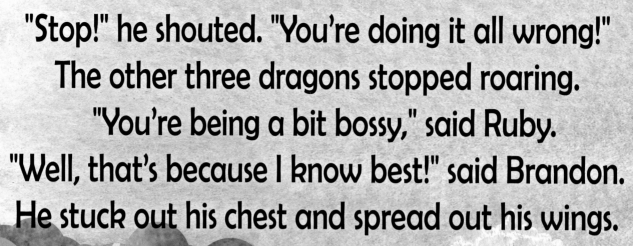

"Stop!" he shouted. "You're doing it all wrong!"
The other three dragons stopped roaring.
"You're being a bit bossy," said Ruby.
"Well, that's because I know best!" said Brandon.
He stuck out his chest and spread out his wings.
"Listen to me!"

His friends listened for a bit, but Brandon wouldn't let them join in. Soon they left him to practice by himself.

When Brandon finished roaring,
he sat down on a rock. The forest was quiet.
He was alone. He wondered what the
others were doing.

Then he noticed smoke in the sky above the trees.
The smoke made different shapes - a butterfly,
a boat, and a banana.

21

STOP!

Brandon followed the smoke shapes.
When he reached a clearing, he saw
his three friends. They were practicing
their fire breathing without him!

"Stop!" he shouted, hurrying towards them.
"You're doing it all wrong! You're blowing
out too much fire! Watch me!"

The other dragons looked at each other.
"We wanted to practice by ourselves," said Noah.
"You're always telling us what to do!"
complained Jasmine.
"You're SO bossy!" added Ruby.

"Oh," said Brandon. Ruby was right.
He'd wanted them to do everything his way.
"I'm sorry I was bossy," he said.
"Jasmine is really good at flying. Noah is great at
roaring and Ruby is fantastic at fire breathing.
You don't need me to tell you what to do."

26

Ruby looked thoughtful for a minute. Then she grinned at Brandon. "OF COURSE we need you!" she cried. "I've just had a brilliant idea!"

27

The next day dawned bright and sunny.
Everyone gathered for the Dragon Skills Contest.
The prizes for flying, roaring, and fire breathing
stood gleaming on a table.

Brandon felt nervous, and excited.
"Are you ready?" whispered Ruby.

Brandon nodded and held up a flag.
"Ready, steady, GO!" he yelled
in his biggest, bossiest voice.

WHOOOOSH!

And this time, his friends did exactly what he told them!

Glossary

annoyed a little mad

brilliant very smart

clearing land cleared of trees and bushes

echo to repeat over and over

gleaming shining with bright light

overhead above one's head

zoom to go speedily

Index

Further Reading

Berry, Joy Wilt. *Being Bossy: A Help Me Be Good Book*. London: Watkins, 2013.

McCall, Gerrie. *Dragons and Serpents*. New York: Gareth Stevens, 2011.

Websites

For web resources related to the subject of this book, go to:
www.windmillbooks.com/weblinks and select this book's title.